Adventures in Ana Park

By TREVON EVANS
and KAHLIYA RUFFIN

Illustrated by LIU LIGHT

Reach Incorporated | Washington, DC
Shout Mouse Press

Reach Education, Inc. / Shout Mouse Press
Published by
Shout Mouse Press, Inc.

Shout Mouse Press is a nonprofit writing and publishing program dedicated to amplifying unheard voices. This book was produced through Shout Mouse writing workshops and in collaboration with Shout Mouse artists and editors.

Shout Mouse Press empowers writers from marginalized communities to tell their own stories in their own voices and, as published authors, to act as agents of change. In partnership with other nonprofit organizations serving communities in need, we are building a catalog of inclusive, mission-driven books that engage reluctant readers as well as open hearts and minds.

Learn more and see our full catalog at www.shoutmousepress.org.

This is for all the kids who love to explore.

Blue sky and bright yellow sun.
It's Saturday afternoon,
no better day for a cookout.
Dad starts up the grill.
Mom says, "Go have fun, kids!
But not too much fun."
Laughter spreads through the air.

We head off
on our own adventure...

First stop, the pirate ship!
Black, red and **HUMONGOUS,**
the ship stands at the center of the park.
Kids sliding, running, using sticks as swords.

Clink Clink Clink!

No one is at the helm,
so we grab the slippery wheel.
We are Captains.
"Yar!" we yell. "Ahoy matey!"
The grass turns to water,
and we set sail...

Our ship slides onto the sand,
and we rush to the building ahead.
The Anacostia Aquatic Center!
We step inside and see the biggest fish.
We cannot believe our eyes.

A huge blue tank in the back
holds Snappy the Turtle.
Snap, snap, snap!
He has dark green skin, sharp claws...

...and a dragon tail!

CLAP ALONG IF YOU FEEL LIKE A ROOM WITHOUT
Anacostia Rollers

ROOF ♪♫ BECAUSE I'M HAPPY ♪♫♪♪♩ CLAP ALONG IF

At the roller skating rink
hip hop beats
burst from the speakers.
We pick up our skates,
sit on the steps, and lace up.

The wind blows in our faces
as we glide smooth and fast.

The tricks! The flips!

A woman wearing a jacket
that says "Anacostia Rollers"
zooms by.

At the courts there are
tall men in tank tops,
balls bouncing and being passed,
gawking faces through the gate.

We imagine ourselves on the team,
Slam Dunking,
    High-Fiving.
The crowd cheers!
We rule the court.

We stroll under the bridge,
and cars pass above.

Vroom vroom!

In the distance,
people in matching shirts
pick up trash
to keep our kingdom clean.

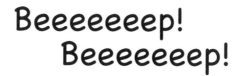

Beeeeeeep!
Beeeeeeep!

A boat floats by,
nets scooping bottles,
so our river can stay beautiful.

Swish! Swish!

Our shoes brush
through dry grass.
A slap on the shoulder.
Tag, you're it!
We run through the park, laughing.

As we run, the sun tags along.
Skrrrt! We stop in our tracks.
A deer runs past.

Look! Up ahead!
A long, wooden dock.
Water ripples against the edge.
Whoosh, whoosh.
We stand and look out.
Boats float on the other side,

Gentle on the waves.
The water is like a mirror,
reflecting the river bank.
For us, the trees are dancing.

As the sun sets,
we go quiet.

Mom calls our names in the distance.
We run back as fast as our legs can go.
Mmmmm! Is that burgers we smell?

Plates already made,
we slide onto the picnic bench.
Before we can even pick up our food...
Swoosh! Caw! Caw!
A seagull steals the chips!
We giggle and keep eating.

Stuffed tummies, sad faces,
we pack up our bags
and walk slowly to the car.

All around us,
the park prepares for night.
Deer, foxes, and bunny rabbits come out.
A Great Blue Heron stands on a post.
Chirp! Chirp! Crickets in the grass.

We bundle together in the backseat.
Our eyes get heavy.

Yawwwnnn.

The light from the moon
reflects on the water
like a flashlight.

Today's adventure is over,
and we slip into our dreams.

About Ana Park

Anacostia Park, sometimes called 'Ana Park' by locals, is a vibrant urban park in Southeast Washington, D.C.

Authors Kahliya and Trevon live nearby and often visit the park. They wanted to celebrate it as a special place, especially because in 2018 Ana Park turns 100 years old!

On August 31, 1918, Congress passed a law to preserve this land along the Anacostia River as recreation space for public use.

Now, 100 years later, D.C. residents like Kahliya and Trevon can go there to picnic, play basketball, roller skate, see nature, relax, and—like the characters in this book—go on adventures.

Happy Birthday, Ana Park!

About the Authors

Trevon Evans

is a senior at Richard Wright Public Charter School. He likes to draw and to play football and basketball. He wants to start playing lacrosse, and in the future he would like to be a visual artist. He wants this book to be something that kids can relate to, especially because many of them know Anacostia Park. The book shows images of kids having fun at the park, and he wants young readers to take away that they should enjoy their childhood.

Kahliya Ruffin

is seventeen years old and is in the 12th grade at Anacostia High School. This is her second children's book with Reach and Shout Mouse Press. Her first book was *Deena Misses Her Mom* (2017). Kahliya's hobbies include boxing and playing basketball. She hopes that children who read this book will realize that there is hidden beauty everywhere.

Holly Bass served as Story Coach for this book.
Hayes Davis served as Head Story Coach for this year's series.

About the Illustrator

Liu Light

Light graduated with a BFA in Painting and Printmaking from Virginia Commonwealth University in 2016. Since graduating, they have been actively involved in the DIY music and art community in Richmond, VA, created music and performed under the moniker Yaya, and curated experimental shows and art projects with two other collaborators in their art space, 3 Moons. They developed a strong interest in and compassion for supporting people, especially youth, who are marginalized by their identities, cultures, and disabilities. Recently, they have rekindled their love for illustration, comics, and animated media, and hope to pursue their talents and passions as far as they can go. See more of their work at: www.liu-light.tumblr.com.

Writers and artists at work

Acknowledgments

For the sixth summer in a row, teens from Reach Incorporated were issued a challenge: compose original children's books that will both educate and entertain young readers. Specifically, these teens were asked to create inclusive stories that reflect the realities of their communities, so that every child has the opportunity to relate to characters on the page. And for the sixth summer in a row, these teens have demonstrated that they know their audience, they believe in their mission, and they take pride in the impact they can make on young lives.

Thirteen writers spent the month of July brainstorming ideas, generating potential plots, writing, revising, and providing critiques. Authoring quality books is challenging work, and these authors have our immense gratitude and respect: Talik, Synia, Jada, Temil, Trevon, Kahliya, De'Asia, India, Essence, Malik, Brittany, Dartavius, and Don'nayah.

These books represent a collaboration between Reach Incorporated and Shout Mouse Press, and we are grateful for the leadership provided by members of both teams. From Reach, John Gass contributed meaningfully to discussions and morale, and the Reach summer program leadership of Luisa Furstenberg-Beckman kept us organized and well-equipped. From the Shout Mouse Press team, we thank Head Story Coach Hayes Davis, who oversaw this year's workshops, and Story Coaches Holly Bass, Sarai Johnson, Barrett Smith, and Eva Shapiro for bringing both fun and insight to the project. We can't thank enough illustrators Jiaqi Zhou, Liu Light, West Cahall, and India Valle for bringing these stories to life with their beautiful artwork. Finally, Amber Colleran brought a keen eye and important mentorship to the project as the series Art Director and book designer. We are grateful for the time and talents of these writers and artists!

Finally, we thank those of you who have purchased books and cheered on our authors. It is your support that makes it possible for these teen authors to engage and inspire young readers. We hope you smile as much while you read as these teens did while they wrote.

Mark Hecker,
Reach Incorporated

Kathy Crutcher,
Shout Mouse Press

About Reach Incorporated

Reach Incorporated develops grade-level readers and capable leaders by preparing teens to serve as tutors and role models for younger students, resulting in improved literacy outcomes for both.

Founded in 2009, Reach recruits high school students to be elementary school reading tutors. Elementary school students average 1.5 grade levels of reading growth per year of participation. This growth – equal to that created by highly effective teachers – is created by high school students who average more than two grade levels of growth per year of program participation.

As skilled xreading tutors, our teens noticed that the books they read with their students did not reflect their reality. As always, we felt the best way we could address this issue was to let our teen tutors author new books themselves. Through our collaboration with Shout Mouse Press, these teens create engaging stories with diverse characters that invite young readers to explore the world through words. By purchasing our books, you support student-led, community-driven efforts to improve educational outcomes in the District of Columbia.

Learn more at reachincorporated.org.

CPSIA information can be obtained
at www.ICGtesting.com
Printed in the USA
LVHW070502271122
733986LV00007B/274